Queen Serena

Lee Aucoin, *Creative Director*
Jamey Acosta, *Senior Editor*
Heidi Fiedler, *Editor*
Produced and designed by
Denise Ryan & Associates
Illustration © Kathy Couri
Rachelle Cracchiolo, *Publisher*

Teacher Created Materials
5301 Oceanus Drive
Huntington Beach, CA 92649-1030
http://www.tcmpub.com
Paperback: ISBN: 978-1-4333-5598-1
Library Binding: ISBN: 978-1-4807-1720-6
© 2014 Teacher Created Materials

Written by
Jordan Moore

Illustrated by
Kathy Couri

D1444663

Contents

Chapter One

The Queen Awakes

Little Miss Serena is a very elegant young lady. Every morning, she brushes her hair one hundred times until it is perfectly silky.

This morning feels different. It feels special. Today is a beautiful day. Rays of light filter through her curtains. They wake her gently. She stretches her arms and gives a little yawn.

Serena loves to wear her shiny pearls. Her closet is full of sparkly dresses. It's difficult for her to choose among the rainbow of colors. For a moment, she stares at her closet before choosing a puffy, purple dress. It's her favorite. It has sequins on the top and spins around her wonderfully when she twirls.

With one light movement, she leaps out of bed and gets dressed. She sings and dances around her room. She makes a lot of noise. Secretly, she hopes her mother will come tell her what a beautiful voice she has. She sings louder and louder and dances with heavier steps.

No one comes, so she descends the stairs so gracefully you might think she is royalty. For today is no ordinary day. It is her birthday.

8

Chapter Two

An Empty Stomach, an Empty Kitchen

Serena sits patiently at the dining table. Her breakfast can't be far away. She spies the little dinner bell. She does not like waiting. *Ding! Ding! Ding!* But no one comes.

"BREAKFAST!" She screams so loudly that the house shakes. But there is only an echo, and then silence. Serena taps her feet. After five l-o-n-g minutes, she stomps into the kitchen.

"MOMMY! WHERE ARE MY PANCAKES?" But no one answers.

Her stomach grumbles. She will have to fix her own food. She opens the fridge. On the bottom shelf, there is a stack of pancakes with a note.

Gone to the store. We saved you some pancakes.

Love, Mom

11

GASP! A queen eats only fresh, hot pancakes. Not cold leftovers.

"If you want something done, you have to do it yourself," says Serena as she lifts an apron carefully over her head and ties it neatly around her waist.

But Serena doesn't know how to cook, especially not pancakes. She smashes some eggs in the bowl, including the eggshells. She pours milk on the counter instead of in the batter. She adds a spoonful (or six) of sugar to the mix. Then, she sprinkles a handful of salt through the air. Clouds of flour fill the kitchen. It's all one big mess.

Serena sighs. This is more difficult than she thought. She takes off her apron, dusts herself off carefully, and then walks outside.

14

Chapter Three

The Garden Beast

Serena wanders out into the garden. She hopes to find someone to pay attention to her. People always listen to her!

Suddenly, a huge figure jumps out of the bushes. It is covered in leaves and dirt. Serena is shocked but not scared. (We all know queens do not get scared.)

"Princess!" the figure cries. "Happy birthday!" Before Serena can protest, he wraps his arms around her in a bear hug.

"DAAAAADDY! You're filthy! Where are my pancakes? Where are my presents? Where is my pony?" she yells, pushing herself free.

"A pony? Keep dreaming, Princess. *Maybe* we'll go to an amusement park," he replies, laughing. "Now, go find your brother. He's been at the neighbors' house all morning."

"An amusement park? Now, that's more like it! When do we leave?" asks Serena, looking hopeful. Her father just laughs and ruffles her hair.

"Off you go, Princess, I have work to do." With that, he disappears from sight. Serena is not impressed.

"Don't call me Princess! I'm a queen!" she cries as she flicks back her hair. She storms off to find her brother Mick at the Maples' house next door.

Chapter Four

The Royal Banquet

The neighbors' door is wide open. Serena stomps down the hallway to find Mick, but pauses at the kitchen.

On the table is an amazing cake. She creeps in for a closer look.

"Don't touch it, Serena!" says Mrs. Maple, coming into the kitchen, "My, you're a mess! What *have* you been doing? Go join the boys in the yard."

Serena looks disappointedly at the cake and continues outside. She hears noises, but Mick is not there. Serena clambers onto the fence to see what is going on. In her yard, there are balloons, tables, chairs, and even a jumping castle. There is so much food that it looks like a banquet! She can't believe her eyes!

"There you are, Princess! I mean our Queen for the Day." Her dad walks toward her, dressed as a knight. He winks and lifts her over the fence. "The royal table awaits, Your Majesty!"

Queen Serena smiles regally and sits at the end of the table. Princes, princesses, and knights surround her. Her face is dirty, and there are leaves in her hair and blobs of batter on her dress. She does not look like a queen. But she is, just for a day.

Jordan Moore lives in Melbourne, Australia. When she's not writing, Jordan paints, draws, plays clarinet and guitar, and plans trips to Paris and Barcelona where she once lived. Jordan wrote *Sinbad the Sailor, The Marshmallow Man,* and *The Mystery of the Grand Bazaar* for Read! Explore! Imagine! Fiction Readers.

Kathy Couri was born in New York, grew up in Columbus, Ohio, and now lives in Kansas. Kathy, who has always loved to draw, illustrates children's books and magazines. When Kathy is not illustrating for children, she collects vintage children's books and toys. Edmund Dulac of France is one of her favorite illustrators.